Garbage Snooper
Surprise

Read other

SPENCER'S
adventures

#1 Stop That Eyeball!
#2 Garbage Snooper Surprise

•••••• coming soon ••••••

#3 Hair in the Air

SPENCER'S adventures

Garbage Snooper Surprise

by

Gary Hogg

illustrated by Chuck Slack

A
LITTLE APPLE
PAPERBACK

SCHOLASTIC INC.
New York   Toronto   London   Auckland   Sydney

For my princess, Annie,
a girl who sparkles with goodness.

ISBN 0-590-93936-X

Text copyright © 1995 by Gary Hogg.
Illustrations copyright © 1996 by Scholastic Inc.
All rights reserved. Published by Scholastic Inc., 555 Broadway, New York, NY 10012.

LITTLE APPLE PAPERBACKS and the LITTLE APPLE PAPERBACKS logo are trademarks of Scholastic Inc.

12 11 10 9 8 7 6 5 4 3 2 1   6 7 8 9/9 0 1/0

Printed in the U.S.A.   40

First Scholastic printing, December 1996

CONTENTS

. . . .

Chapter One

Trash Dash

"Oh no!" cried Spencer as he peered out the living room window. It looked like a garbage bomb had exploded on the front lawn. Trash was scattered from one end of the yard to the other.

"Why do I have to be in charge of the stupid garbage?" moaned Spencer.

"It's not fair. Just once I wish I could be in charge of something good, like cleaning out the cookie jar."

1

Spencer glanced at the clock and started to panic. The garbage truck would be arriving any minute. The pressure was on. He had to get that mess cleaned up fast.

Spencer ran to his sister's room and knocked loudly on the door.

"Who's there?" called Amber.

"It's me, Spencer."

"Go away!" she yelled back.

Spencer gritted his teeth. "Listen, Amber, I need help. The garbage is all over the yard and the truck will be here any minute. Will you please help me clean it up?"

"What will you give me if I do? And it better be good."

Spencer did some quick addition in his head. "How about 36 cents?"

"Not even close," Amber hooted. "I meant something like this: I help you clean up the stinking mess and you move to Brazil."

"Very funny," said Spencer.

"OK, I'll help you if you promise to do the dishes all by yourself for the next three years."

"Just forget it!" shouted Spencer. As usual, his sister had turned out to be no help at all. He would have to tackle this mess all by himself.

"Ladies and gentlemen," announced Spencer. "Welcome to the 100-yard trash dash. Our first contestant is Speedy Spencer. Please, don't blink or you might miss him."

Speedy Spencer jumped off the porch and started grabbing garbage. He whirled around the yard like a tornado sucking up trash. He stuffed armful after armful into the garbage cans.

Finally, Spencer crammed the lid on

the last can and collapsed on the grass. The trash dash had left him completely exhausted.

Spencer was still stretched out next to the cans when the garbage men arrived.

"Look, Earl," said the skinny man, pointing at Spencer. "Someone has thrown away a perfectly good kid."

"Yeah," replied Earl. "It's a shame we have to take him to the dump."

"Hey, wait a minute," exclaimed Spencer, jumping to his feet.

The men looked at each other and started to laugh.

"What are you doing out here with the trash?" asked the skinny man.

"I was cleaning up the yard," explained Spencer. "Something knocked the garbage cans over and made the biggest mess you've ever seen."

Earl scratched his head. "Sounds like you've got a Garbage Snooper."

"A what?" asked Spencer.

"A Garbage Snooper," said the skinny man. "A Snoop digs through people's trash looking for treasures."

"We don't have any treasures in our trash," said Spencer.

"Well, one man's trash is another man's treasure," laughed Earl as he emptied the last can into the truck. "Your Snoop will probably keep coming back every garbage day until you catch him."

"And how am I supposed to do that?"

Earl gave Spencer a big wink. "I'm sure a smart boy like you will think of something," he said. Both men jumped on the truck, and it headed down the street.

Spencer waved good-bye and then dragged the empty cans back to the garage.

Chapter Two

To Snag a Snoop

"Mom, where are you?" shouted Spencer as he entered the house.

"I'm in the laundry room," replied Mrs. Burton.

Spencer burst through the door like a firecracker. "Mom, we've got big trouble," he blurted out.

"Calm down, Spencer," said his mother. "If you want to talk about trouble, we can discuss these smelly socks."

"Stinking socks are nothing compared to what I have to tell you." Spencer's eyes grew even bigger as he took a deep breath and announced, "Mom, we have a Snarbage Gooper."

"A what?" she asked.

"I mean a Garbage Snooper," corrected Spencer. "He snooped our garbage this morning and made the biggest mess you ever saw. Earl said we have to catch him."

"Oh, I don't know the first thing about Snooper catching."

"That's OK, because I've got some great ideas," said Spencer. "We can hook the garbage cans up to an electric wire. The second the Snoop starts his dirty work, *zap,* he gets fried."

"I don't want any fried Snoopers on

the lawn. What would the neighbors think?"

"Well, what if I dig a big pit next to the garbage cans and build a trap door over it. When he gets near the cans, *whoosh,* down he goes. We could keep him in the pit for a few days until he's ready to talk."

"Talk about what?" asked his mother.

"About where he's stashed the loot."

"Honey, if this gooper has some of our garbage stashed someplace, it's perfectly fine with me. I don't want any pits in the yard. What if your father fell in? On second thought, maybe a pit wouldn't be such a bad idea," she said, laughing.

"Then it's OK?" asked Spencer excitedly.

"No, Spencer. Absolutely no deep pits in the yard."

"If I can't fry him or trap him in a pit, how do you expect me to catch him?"

"Why don't you just write a little note asking him to stop? You could tape it to one of the garbage cans."

Spencer could see it was no use talking to his mom. She was way too nice. If Jack the Ripper showed up at their house, she would probably give him cookies and offer him a job sharpening knives.

When Spencer heard his dad's car pull into the driveway, he ran out to meet him.

"Guess what, Dad? We have a Garbage Snooper," said Spencer. "Do I have your permission to catch him? I promise I won't dig any pits or hook any electric wires to the garbage cans."

"Slow down a minute," said Mr. Burton, lifting his golf clubs out of the trunk. "What makes you think we have a Garbage Snooper?"

"Because this morning our garbage was all over the yard. Earl and the other guy said it sounded like the work of a Snooper."

"It sounds like the work of a dog to me," said Spencer's dad. "But if you want to try to catch him, go right ahead."

"Thanks, Dad," said Spencer. "I won't let you down."

Chapter Three

Two Heads Are Better Than One

"I need to do some serious thinking," said Spencer as he sat down at his desk. He opened the top drawer and pulled out a stack of comic books.

"Maybe these will inspire me," he said, thumbing through the books. "These superhero guys have it easy. If I could stretch my neck like Pencilneck or fly and sting like Bee Boy, that Snooper would be no problem."

Spencer put his feet up on the desk, leaned back in his chair, and closed his eyes. He started daydreaming that he was Pencilneck.

In his dream, he stretched his neck all the way down the hall and into Amber's room. His neck pushed his head along the floor and under Amber's bed.

When Amber sat down on her bed, Spencer's neck stretched even farther and his head shot up right next to Amber.

Amber screamed and tried to run, but Spencer wrapped his neck around her leg.

"Not so fast, you big pain in the neck. You better pack a few things before you leave. After all, you are going all the way to Brazil."

Spencer's daydream was interrupted by his mother. "Spencer, the phone is for you. It's Josh."

Grabbing the phone, Spencer blurted out, "Hey Josh, I just found out that we have a Garbage Snooper."

"You have a Garbage Snooper?" gasped Josh. "Wow! Unbelievable! Awesome! You lucky dog! Um, what's a Garbage Snooper?"

"It's kind of like a werewolf, but instead of ripping out your guts, it rips through your garbage."

"Does it eat your garbage?" asked Josh.

"I'm not sure," said Spencer. "But Snoopers are very dangerous and I'm going to catch this one all by myself."

"Let me help," begged Josh.

"No way," insisted Spencer. "This is serious business and you might get hurt."

"I have a box of chocolates that my grandma gave me," said Josh. "I'll share them with you."

"The candy your grandma gives you is always old and gross."

"These are good," said Josh. "They haven't even turned gray. My grandpa took a few sample bites out of some of them, but other than that, they're in great shape."

"Well," said Spencer, "chocolate is excellent brain food and two heads are better than one. All right, come on over."

Josh flew down the street on his bike. Soon he was at Spencer's door. The boys flopped down on the bed and began munching the brain food.

"Do you know where we can get a couple of grenades?" asked Spencer.

"No, but I know how to make a stink bomb."

"A good stink would be nice, but I think it will take more than that to stop this Snooper."

"How about a giant mousetrap?" asked Josh. "Do you think the Snooper likes cheese?"

"No, he just likes garbage. Hey, wait a minute, that's it!" exclaimed Spencer.

"What?" puzzled Josh.

Spencer sat up straight and started to talk fast. "The one thing we know for sure is that the Snooper loves garbage. So, let's give him some garbage that he'll never forget."

"What on earth are you talking about?"

"I'm talking about disguising myself as a pile of garbage. That way, when he starts snooping in our trash, I'll be right there to snag him."

"Oh, now I get it," said Josh. "It's brilliant! But where are we going to get a garbage disguise?"

"We'll make it," said Spencer. "Garbage day isn't until next Saturday. That gives us a whole week to collect trash for the garbage suit.

"Start hiding all of your family's garbage under your bed. On Friday, bring it over to my house and we'll use it to build the costume."

"Excellent," said Josh. "We'll give this Garbage Snooper the biggest surprise of his life."

Chapter Four

Stinkman Meets Megamom

Friday afternoon, Josh showed up at Spencer's house with three bags full of garbage.

"Hello, Josh," said Spencer's dad as he opened the door. "What have you got there?"

"Oh, nothing, just some old garbage."

"Well, you can never have too much garbage," laughed Mr. Burton. "Spencer is in his room. Go on in."

Josh gave three short raps and two hard knocks on Spencer's door. That was their secret code.

"Bah, bah, black sheep, have you any trash?" whispered Spencer through the door.

"Yes sir, yes sir, three bags full," replied Josh.

The door flew open. "Good work," said Spencer. "Did you have any trouble?"

"No, but my mom almost fainted when she saw me taking out the trash without being asked."

Josh opened the bags and poured the garbage onto Spencer's bed.

"Whew," gasped Spencer. "That stuff really stinks."

"Of course it stinks," replied Josh. "Now, how are we going to make it stick to you?"

"That's what these are for," said

Spencer, pointing to a box containing wire, a stapler, tape, glue, and some nails. "We only use the nails if we absolutely have to."

"Right," said Josh, picking up the first chunk of junk.

Spencer stood as still as a statue while Josh blanketed him with trash.

Soon his shirt was loaded with crumpled newspaper, spoiled food, and eggshells. His pants were adorned with banana peels, cans, bottles, and a pair of worn-out shoes.

Josh cut three holes in a cereal box and shoved it over Spencer's head.

"How do I look?" asked Spencer.

"You look gross and disgusting and you smell even worse," replied Josh.

"Great," said Spencer, very pleased. "Now all I need is an awesome name like other superheroes have."

"We could call you Garboman," suggested Josh.

"No," said Spencer. "We need something tougher."

"How about Captain Trashmasher?" offered Josh.

"You're getting closer, but you're not there yet."

Josh picked up a slimy, smelly banana peel. "What about Stinkman?"

"Bingo!" said Spencer. "That's who I am, Stinkman, Fearless Protector of Garbage."

Spencer and Josh were startled by a knock on the bedroom door.

"Boys," called Mrs. Burton, "what's going on in there? A very bad smell is coming from this room."

"Don't worry, Mom. It's just Josh. He's not feeling all that great."

"Yeah," groaned Josh. "I feel kind of sick."

"Oh dear," said Mrs. Burton. "I better call your mother."

"No, please don't. This happens to me all the time. I smell pretty bad, but I'll be fine."

"I better have a look at you," she insisted. When the door swung open, Mrs. Burton stared at the garbage in horror.

"What on earth is going on here?" she gasped. "Joshua, where is Spencer?"

Stinkman didn't move a single muscle. What good is a great disguise if you don't use it?

"I've got to go home now," said Josh. "It's way past my bedtime."

"Josh, it is only 4:30 in the afternoon. I think you'd better stay right here until I find out what's going on. Now, where is Spencer?"

Josh gave up and pointed at Stinkman. "He's right there."

"Don't be ridiculous. That is just a pile of disgusting garbage."

"No, really, that's Spencer. We made a garbage suit so he could catch the Snooper."

Spencer's mother walked over and looked closely at Stinkman. "Spencer, are you in there?"

Stinkman was thinking fast. He had seen that look in his mother's eyes many times. It always meant trouble. Spencer figured this would be a good time to check out Stinkman's superhuman powers.

Spencer turned and took a flying leap out of his open window. He landed in a perfect bellyflop on the flower bed. Flying obviously wasn't one of

Stinkman's special powers.

As he got to his feet, he detected a loud growling sound. "I hope I have superhuman hearing," gasped Spencer. "Because if I don't, there is one very large dog growling right at me."

Spencer was wrong. There were two very large dogs growling right at him. The Petersons' German shepherds were looking Stinkman over and licking their chops.

It wasn't much of a chase. Supersonic speed wasn't one of Stinkman's powers either. He waddled down the sidewalk like a big smelly duck, with two German shepherds barking and nipping at his heels.

Suddenly Spencer stopped. "Hey, I don't have to put up with this," he said. "I'm a superhero." He spun around and faced the dogs.

Spencer reached down and pulled a

half-eaten ham sandwich off of his chest. He threw the sandwich into the flower bed and the dogs raced after it.

"Those fleabags are no match for Stinkman," said Spencer.

On his way back to the house, Stinkman came eye to eye with the world's mightiest superhero.

Stronger than a smelly diaper. Faster than a speeding two-year-old. Able to leap piles of laundry in a single bound. It was Megamom!

Mrs. Burton used her superhuman powers to convince Josh and Spencer to lay Stinkman to rest. The boys peeled the layers of garbage off of Spencer and filled a trash can with them.

Mrs. Burton observed the entire process with her hands on her hips.

"Now, take off that shirt and throw it

away, too. I don't even want to think about washing it."

"But Mom," Spencer protested. "This is my Famous Potato shirt from Idaho. It's the only one like it in the whole school."

Megamom raised one of her powerful eyebrows and Spencer dropped the shirt in the garbage.

Josh went home and Spencer went to bed. It didn't bother him to go to bed so early. What bothered him was that the Garbage Snooper was about to strike again and there wasn't anything he could do about it.

Chapter Five

Wanted: Garbage Snooper

"**S**pencer!" called Mr. Burton. "The garbage cans are tipped over again and the yard is covered with trash. Hurry and get it cleaned up before the truck comes."

Spencer grumbled and growled as he attacked the mess. In every piece of trash, he pictured the Snooper's face. He kicked cans. He ripped papers. He smashed cartons.

The screech of the garbage truck's brakes brought Spencer to his senses.

"Whoa, big guy," said Earl. "What in tarnation has got you all riled up?"

"It's that Snooper," said Spencer. "He's driving me crazy."

"You should ask around," said the skinny man, lifting a trash can onto his shoulder. "I'll bet some of your neighbors are having the same trouble. Maybe they could help you catch this Snooper."

"That's a fantastic idea," said Spencer. "I'll make some wanted posters and put them up around town."

"That's the spirit," said Earl, emptying the last can into the truck.

Right after breakfast, Spencer got out his art supplies and went to work.

At the top of a clean piece of white paper he wrote, "WANTED: GARBAGE SNOOPER." Below that he printed,

"This ruthless criminal has been digging through people's garbage without even asking. He leaves behind really big messes. He must be stopped. If you have any information about this creep, call Spencer at 776-9832."

"Now all I need is a picture," said Spencer. He went to the kitchen and got the morning paper.

On the front page, he found a picture of a man holding a piece of garbage. "Now this sleazy guy looks exactly like a Snooper to me," thought Spencer.

He laid the wanted poster over the newspaper and began tracing the face of the man in the picture.

Spencer didn't take time to read the caption below the photograph. It read, "Mayor Jensen kicks off annual clean-up week by throwing in first piece of trash."

Spencer spent almost an hour tracing every detail of the mayor's face. He wanted it to be perfect.

The man at Pro Print Copy Shop was so busy, he made Spencer's twelve copies without even looking at the poster.

Spencer hung one in the post office and taped others in store windows. He kept one poster to show to the neighbors.

The first house Spencer stopped at was the Hiskeys'. Mr. Hiskey opened the door. "Hello, Spencer. What can I do for you?"

"I'm on official business today," said Spencer, holding up the poster. "I'm trying to catch a Garbage Snooper. He's been ripping through our garbage every Saturday and making a big mess. I want to catch him and I hope you can help me."

Mr. Hiskey took the poster and studied it carefully. "You know," he said softly. "This face looks familiar. I'm sure I've seen it before."

Spencer started to get excited. "Think, Mr. Hiskey," he said. "Think real hard."

Mr. Hiskey bit his lip and squinted one eye. He was thinking as hard as he could.

Mrs. Hiskey came into the room and looked over her husband's shoulder. "That's a very good drawing of the mayor," she said. "Did you draw it all by yourself, Spencer?"

Mr. Hiskey let out a gasp. "So the mayor has been snooping through garbage cans. I knew he was a crook all along."

"But honey, didn't you vote for him?" asked Mrs. Hiskey.

"Sneaking around and digging in garbage is not the American way," spluttered Mr. Hiskey. "I'm going down to city hall right now."

Spencer jumped on his bike and rode home as fast as he could. He could hardly wait to tell his parents the big news.

"You will never guess who has been digging in our garbage," shouted Spencer as he raced through the front door.

"Well, Spencer, let me try," said his mother. "How about the mayor?"

Spencer stopped dead in his tracks. "How did you know?"

"He is on the phone with your father right now."

"So, he called to turn himself in," said Spencer.

"Not exactly," sighed Mrs. Burton.

Spencer went into the kitchen, where his dad was on the phone. Mr. Burton's face was very red and there was sweat running down his forehead.

"We are very sorry. Yes, I know that it's not true. Of course, you have better things to do than look through our garbage. We will take all of the posters down immediately. Yes sir, I will have a long talk with him. Good-bye."

Spencer's dad hung up the phone and Spencer hung down his head.

Chapter Six

Total Jerk

Spencer thought the weekend would never end. After taking down the wanted posters, he had to stay in his room and write a three-page letter of apology to the mayor.

It was a relief to go back to school Monday morning. As Spencer entered the school yard, he was met by a very excited Josh Porter.

"It's here," exclaimed Josh.

"What's here?" asked Spencer.

"Your potato shirt that you threw away Friday is here."

"Are you sure?"

"Sure, I'm sure. I saw it with my own eyes. That new kid, T.J. Powell, is wearing it."

Spencer ran to the classroom. He took out a pencil and went to the front of the room to sharpen it. As he turned the handle on the pencil sharpener, he looked down the row to T.J.'s desk.

T.J. was bent over, tying knots in his broken shoelaces. When Spencer finally got a good look at T.J.'s shirt, the eyes of two famous potatoes were looking back at him. Josh was right. It was his Idaho shirt.

Spencer went back to his desk. The rest of the morning, he couldn't concentrate on any of his schoolwork. All he could think about was T.J. and his shirt.

When the recess bell rang, Spencer was out of his seat in a flash. He cracked his knee on a chair as he raced to meet Josh. He started hopping on one leg, while holding the knee in his hands.

He hopped right past T.J. "Are you all right?" asked T.J. as Spencer bounced by.

"None of your business," snorted Spencer.

Josh and Spencer put their heads together as they walked to the playground.

"I'm calling the police," said Spencer.

"Not yet," replied Josh. "What if he's not the right guy? Maybe his grandma is the real Snooper and she just gave the shirt to T.J."

"You're right," said Spencer. "I better feel him out first."

Spencer walked over to where T.J. was drawing something in the dirt with a stick.

"What are you drawing?" asked Spencer.

"None of your business," said T.J.

"It looks like a garbage can to me," said Spencer slyly.

"A garbage can?" laughed T.J. "It's a rocket ship."

"That's too bad, because I am really into garbage," said Spencer. "I like everything about it. The way it sounds when it hits the can. The way it looks, feels, and even smells. I guess you could say that I'm pretty much a garbage kind of guy."

"Sounds to me like you're pretty much a weird kind of guy," said T.J.

"Want to hear a good joke? It's about garbage."

"Sure," said Spencer.

"What do you get if you cross a nut with a bag of garbage?"

"I don't know," said Spencer.

"You get *you*," laughed T.J. as he got up and started to run.

"That's not funny!" yelled Spencer as T.J. ran into the classroom.

Spencer stopped at the door, where Josh was waiting for him.

"I found out what T.J. stands for," said Spencer.

"What's that?" asked Josh.

"Total jerk," replied Spencer.

At lunch, T.J. was seated across from Spencer and Josh. "That surprises me," he said, looking at Spencer's lunch.

"What surprises you?" asked Josh.

"I thought Spencer would have a big

plate of garbage for lunch," laughed T.J.

Josh was laughing, too, until he saw Spencer glaring at him.

Spencer leaned over and whispered into Josh's ear, "Don't get too friendly. Remember, he could be the Snooper."

"I don't care," whispered Josh. "I think he's funny."

"Hey," said T.J. "what are you guys whispering about?"

"Spencer was just saying that he liked your shirt. He was wondering where you got it."

"This ugly shirt? My uncle from Idaho sent it to me. Spencer, if you like it so much, maybe I'll give it to you."

"No way," snapped Spencer. "I would never wear something as ugly as that."

"I'll take it," blurted Josh.

"OK," said T.J. pulling the shirt off

and handing it to Josh. "Now, give me your shirt."

Josh pulled off his shirt and gave it to T.J.

Spencer got up and walked out. "You two make me sick," he said as he left.

"First, he messes up my garbage and now he is messing up my best friend," fumed Spencer.

Chapter Seven

Australian Snooper

That night Spencer called Josh on the phone. "What on earth are you doing? Pretty soon he'll have you snooping through garbage cans with him."

"I don't think he's the Snooper," said Josh. "He's a really nice guy. We're going to the city's annual clean-up this Saturday. Why don't you come with us?"

"No way," snapped Spencer.

"Come on, everyone who shows up at the park with a bag filled with trash gets a free movie ticket. The kid who collects the most garbage gets $10.00 and a special certificate from the mayor."

"The only ticket T.J. will be getting is a one-way ticket to jail," said Spencer. "I'll prove to you and everyone else in the park on Saturday that T.J. Powell is nothing but a lowdown Garbage Snooper."

Spencer hung up the phone. He was still steaming when his mother called to him.

"Spencer, I'm taking Amber to the library. Do you want to come?"

"Yeah, sure," said Spencer.

When Spencer entered the library, he headed straight for the reference desk.

Mrs. Pedler, the head librarian, spotted him. "Is there a certain kind of book that I can help you find?"

"Do you have any books on Snoopers?" asked Spencer.

"That would be in the pet section," she said, as she headed down the row. "Oh, I just love Australian Snoopers. They are the cutest little fellows."

"Huh?" replied Spencer.

"It's so funny the way they wag their little tails and spin around in circles. How long have you had your Snooper?"

"Just a couple of weeks," said Spencer.

"Is he housebroken?"

"What?"

"You know, does he still make messes?"

"Oh yeah," said Spencer. "He makes really big messes."

"You should try bopping him on the nose with a rolled-up newspaper."

"What if he bops me back?" asked Spencer.

"Oh, your little guy sounds unruly. Maybe you should tie him up to a tree in your backyard."

"Now you're talking," said Spencer. "How long should I leave him tied up?"

"However long it takes. My sister Shirley has to keep her Snooper tied up almost all the time."

Spencer couldn't believe his ears. He knew that Mrs. Pedler was strict, but this was ridiculous.

"Here we are," she said, stopping in front of a row of books about dogs. "Now, let's see. You said that you had an Australian Snooper."

"Not an Australian Snooper, a Garbage Snooper."

"Well, whatever kind of dog he is,

you should be able to find him in one of these books."

"He's not a dog. He's a boy," said Spencer. But Mrs. Pedler had already rushed off to help someone else.

Looking for his mother, Spencer came across Mr. Hiskey. He was sitting at a table with a tall stack of books in front of him.

"Hi, Mr. Hiskey. What are you reading?" asked Spencer.

"I'm brushing up on my spying techniques. You were really onto something the other day. The mayor is up to no good and I'm going to find out what it is."

"You're going to spy on the mayor?" asked Spencer.

"Shhh, not so loud," whispered Mr. Hiskey. "Let's just say I'm going to keep an eye on him."

"Do these books tell you how to keep an eye on him?" asked Spencer, picking up a book entitled *Brown's Guide to Surveillance Photography*.

"That's a good one," replied Mr. Hiskey. "It shows how to take someone's picture when they're least expecting it."

"Do you think you could help me get a picture of T.J. Powell when he raids our garbage cans Saturday morning?"

"This Saturday is out. The mayor is going to be at the park giving some award for cleaning up the city. I'll be there with my eyes and ears wide open.

"But I'll tell you what. You can use my old XL246 camera. It's not as good as my new XL600, but it will work for what you want to do."

"Awesome!" said Spencer.

Chapter Eight

One Hour Photo

Friday evening, Mr. Hiskey helped Spencer get everything ready. While Spencer put the garbage cans on the curb, Mr. Hiskey tried to find the best angle to take the pictures.

"This will work," he said, jumping into the bush on the corner of the yard. "Hand me the camera and the tripod."

Mr. Hiskey set the camera on the tripod and pointed it at the garbage cans.

He took an extension cord and connected one end to the camera and the other end to one of the garbage cans.

"Now, when your man grabs the can, it will tug on this line and, *pow*, the camera will automatically start taking pictures. It's as easy as taking candy from a baby."

"You mean as easy as taking garbage from a Snooper," laughed Spencer.

The next morning, Spencer received his usual Saturday morning wake-up call.

"Spencer," his dad said, opening the bedroom door, "you better get up. Something did a number on the garbage cans again."

"Wonderful," said Spencer excitedly as he jumped from his bed.

"Are you feeling OK?" asked Mr. Burton.

"Couldn't be better," said Spencer as

he threw on his clothes. He raced out of the house to the mess waiting for him.

Spencer quickly picked up the garbage and then climbed into the bush.

"I hope the XL246 caught it all on film," said Spencer.

Sure enough, three pictures had been taken. Spencer rewound the film and took it out of the camera.

"Mr. T.J. Smartypants won't be quite so smart when he sees what's on this film."

Spencer put the film in his pocket and ran over to Mr. Hiskey's house.

Mrs. Hiskey answered the door. "Hi, Spencer, have you drawn any more pictures of the mayor?"

"Nope. That last one got me into enough trouble to last for awhile. Is Mr. Hiskey home?"

"I'm afraid you just missed him. He

went to that clean-up celebration they're having at the park."

Spencer handed her the camera and tripod. "Mr. Hiskey let me borrow these."

"I'll tell him you brought them back the minute he gets home."

"Thanks," said Spencer, and he dashed home. When he entered the house he was met by the smell of pancakes cooking.

"Spencer, sit down and eat your breakfast right now," said his mother.

Spencer plopped down and began stuffing sticky pancakes into his mouth. He tried to say something, but his mouth was so full he could only mumble.

"Gross," said Amber. "Mom, Spencer is talking with his mouth full and it's making me sick."

Spencer took a big swig of milk and

tried again. "Mother, may I please ride my bike to the park for the clean-up celebration? Josh is going to be there."

"I think that would be nice. In fact, I think the rest of the family will come over in a little while, so watch for us."

"OK, Mom," said Spencer, heading for his room. He took his money jar out of his underwear drawer and emptied it on his bed.

There were five wadded-up dollar bills and a bunch of change. I hope this is enough, thought Spencer.

He filled his pockets with the money and headed out.

Spencer jumped on his bike and steered it toward Miller's Drugstore. They had a machine that could develop film in one hour.

While Spencer was waiting for the film to develop, a large group of people walked by the store. They were all carrying bags of trash.

"There goes the mayor," said the lady behind the counter. "The celebration at the park must be about to start."

"Can you make that machine go any faster?" asked Spencer.

"No, it takes a full sixty minutes to do the processing," replied the lady.

It seemed like forever, but finally, she called Spencer. "Your pictures are ready. It will be $7.67."

Spencer gave her the five dollars and started counting out the change. By the time he counted out the entire amount, Spencer could hear the band playing over at the park.

"Oh no, it's starting," said Spencer as he ran out the door.

He jumped on his bike and raced to the park.

Chapter Nine

The Envelope Please

When Spencer pulled up to the park, a large group of people were gathering in front of the outdoor stage.

Sitting in a tree with his XL600 focused on the mayor was Mr. Hiskey. Below the tree stood T.J. and Josh. They had at least ten bags of trash beside them.

Josh spotted Spencer and yelled, "T.J. collected the most garbage. He is going to get the certificate and money."

"We'll see about that," said Spencer to himself.

"There you are," said Spencer's mother, walking up to him. Mr. Burton, Amber, and his little brother Jake were with her.

"Where's your bag of trash?" asked Mr. Burton.

"It's around here somewhere," said Spencer. Just then the mayor stood up to the microphone.

Spencer knew this was his chance. He shoved his way to the front and climbed onto the stage with the mayor.

The mayor was startled. "Who are you and what's this all about?" he demanded.

"I'm Spencer. You know, the one who put your picture on the wanted poster.

"In this envelope, I have pictures of the real Garbage Snooper. You have to

look at them before you announce the winner of the contest."

The audience inched closer to the stage to see what Spencer had in the envelope.

"Son, we don't have time for this now," said the mayor.

"Go ahead and open it," someone shouted from the crowd.

"Yeah, we want to see what the boy has," another man called out.

"OK," said the mayor reluctantly. "Ladies and gentlemen, as some of you know, my face appeared on some posters recently. They gave the mistaken idea that I had been snooping in garbage cans.

"Well, this is the young man who created those posters. Now he says that the pictures in this envelope reveal the real Garbage Snooper. So, if you will bear with me, I will open the envelope."

The crowd grew quiet as the mayor took the package from Spencer. The only sound that could be heard was the clicking of Mr. Hiskey's camera.

Spencer stared at T.J. He couldn't wait to see the look on his face when the mayor showed everyone the pictures.

The mayor looked at the photographs and his eyes grew big. He paused for a moment and then said, "These pictures are too blurry. I can't tell who or what it is."

Sheriff Rowlan walked over and took the photos. "Why, Mayor, these are as clear as can be. This is a picture of your dog Roscoe digging in some garbage."

The mayor's face turned red and the entire audience burst into laughter.

Spencer felt stunned as he stepped off the stage. How could he have been so wrong?

As he walked away, Spencer heard the mayor announcing that T.J. Powell was the winner of the garbage collecting contest.

Spencer picked up his bike and started to get on it.

"Hey, Spencer," called Josh. "Aren't you going to the movie with us?"

"I can't," said Spencer.

"Why not?" asked Josh.

"I don't have a ticket. I don't have any money and T.J. hates my guts."

"T.J. doesn't hate your guts. It was his idea to invite you. He said that with the ten dollars he won, he could buy you a ticket and still have enough money left to buy us all treats."

Just then, T.J. came running over

waving his certificate. "Hey guys, I want you to meet my dad."

Spencer could hardly believe his eyes. Standing right beside T.J. was Earl the garbage man.

"It looks like you finally caught your Garbage Snooper," said Earl. "I wish I had a picture of the mayor's face when he found out that his dog was the culprit."

Spencer glanced up and waved at Mr. Hiskey in the tree. "Oh, I think I know where I can get you that picture," he said, smiling.

About the Author

Gary Hogg has always loved stories and has been creating them since he was a boy growing up in Idaho.

Gary is also a very popular storyteller. Each year he brings his humorous tales to life for thousands of people around the United States.

He lives in Huntsville, Utah, with his wife Sherry and their children, Jackson, Jonah, Annie, and Boone.

Here's a sneak peek
at the next

SPENCER'S
adventures

#3 Hair in the Air
by Gary Hogg

Whoosh! The weight of the pouncing cat forced the air out of Spencer. He tried to yell "Cat attack!" but just a whisper whimpered out. And then suddenly, with a gasp, air flooded back into Spencer and the chase was on.

It was Snickers in the lead followed by Spencer. And around the magazine rack they went.

It was Snickers ahead by two lengths.

Spencer was coming on strong as they rounded the bend and headed into the kitchen. The cat scrambled under the table and behind the chair.

They were neck and neck as they entered the home stretch. It looked like it was going to be a photo finish.

Suddenly Snickers disappeared into Grandpa and Grandma's bedroom. Spencer had never been into Grandpa's bedroom before. He was not allowed. But he had to get the cat.

Grandpa would understand. After all, the cat had taken a cheap shot. Grandpa wouldn't want him to get away with something as dirty as that. Slowly, Spencer entered the room. He would just get the cat and get out.

"Here, Snickers," said Spencer. "Come to your pal Spence. I have a little surprise for you."

Spencer looked in the closet. "Kitty,

kitty, kitty." Spencer looked under the bed. "Kitty, kitty, kitty." Spencer looked behind the chair. "Kitty, kitty, kitty." Spencer looked everywhere. Finally he shouted, "Where are you, you crazy cat?"

And as Spencer turned around, there it was. It was brown. It was hairy. It was Grandpa's toupee.

A toupee is a wig. But Grandpa wouldn't let anyone call it a wig. "Wigs are for women," he would always say.

Grandpa called his hair a rug. He said he didn't wear it because he was bald. He wore it to keep his head warm. Sometimes it kept his head so warm that he would sweat. Once he sweated so much that his rug slid right off his head.

Spencer had seen Grandpa without his hair many times. But this was the first time he had ever seen Grandpa's hair without Grandpa.

"I have always wanted to touch this,"

said Spencer as he poked the toupee.

"It feels kind of crusty and stiff. He must use staples or tape to keep it on," thought Spencer. Then he remembered the time he stuck a staple into his finger. Boy, did that hurt. "I'll bet he uses tape."

Spencer lifted up Grandpa's hair and placed it on his head. He looked in the mirror, pretending he was Grandpa. He began to say things he wished Grandpa would say.

"Spencer, you are my favorite grandson. I hate your sister. Here's fifty dollars and the car keys. Go and have some fun."

Then Spencer started to laugh. He laughed so hard that he doubled over and the toupee fell off of his head.

As Spencer reached for the toupee, Snickers suddenly appeared. He began pawing at the wig.

"Oh, you like Grandpa's hair," said

Spencer. He shook the toupee faster and faster in front of Snickers.

Snickers' paws worked like lightning trying to snag the toupee. "Hey, wait a minute," said Spencer. "I have an idea for a great game."